Acting Edition

The Best We Could

(a family tragedy)

by Emily Feldman

No one shall make any changes in this title(s) for the purpose of production. No part of this book may be reproduced, stored in a retrieval system, scanned, uploaded, or transmitted in any form, by any means, now known or yet to be invented, including mechanical, electronic, digital, photocopying, recording, videotaping, or otherwise, without the prior written permission of the publisher. No one shall share this title(s), or any part of this title(s), through any social media or file hosting websites.

For all inquiries regarding motion picture, television, online/digital and other media rights, please contact Concord Theatricals Corp.

MUSIC AND THIRD-PARTY MATERIALS USE NOTE

Licensees are solely responsible for obtaining formal written permission from copyright owners to use copyrighted music and/or other copyrighted third-party materials (e.g. artworks, logos) in the performance of this play and are strongly cautioned to do so. If no such permission is obtained by the licensee, then the licensee must use only original music and materials that the licensee owns and controls. Licensees are solely responsible and liable for clearances of all third-party copyrighted materials, including without limitation music, and shall indemnify the copyright owners of the play(s) and their licensing agent, Concord Theatricals Corp., against any costs, expenses, losses and liabilities arising from the use of such copyrighted third-party materials by licensees. For music, please contact the appropriate music licensing authority in your territory for the rights to any incidental music.

IMPORTANT BILLING AND CREDIT REQUIREMENTS

If you have obtained performance rights to this title, please refer to your licensing agreement for important billing and credit requirements.

THE BEST WE COULD was first produced by the The Manhattan Theatre Club in New York City on March 7, 2023. The performance was directed by Daniel Aukin with choreography by Sunny Hitt, set design by Lael Jellinek, costumes by Anita Yavitch, lighting design by Matt Frey, and sound design by Kate Marvin. The Production Stage Manager was lark hackshaw. The cast was as follows:

MAPS	Maureen Sebastian
ELLA	Aya Cash
PEG	Constance Shulman
LOU	Frank Wood
MARC	Brian D. Coats

This play was made possible with support from SPACE on Ryder Farm, The Cape Cod Theatre Project, Page 73, La Jolla Playhouse, New York Stage and Film, MacDowell, The Edgerton Foundation, and The Tow Foundation.

Additional thanks to Emily Simoness, Joshua Brody, Michael Walkup, Kate Eminger, and most especially Daniel Aukin.

CHARACTERS

MAPS – A woman.

ELLA – A woman.

PEG – A woman, Ella's mother.

LOU – A man, Ella's father.

MARC – A man, a contemporary of Lou and Peg.

There is some flexibility in age for all of the characters. Ella's line "Actually, I'm thirty-six" can be adjusted to reflect the age of the actor playing the role.

AUTHOR'S NOTES

A bare stage is all you need.

The places, things, and even the dog can live in the audience's imagination.

Time slips forward and backward with fluid transitions.

For my parents.

(**MAPS** *enters and begins the play when she is ready.*)

MAPS. We're about to get started here.

Could we take some of these lights down a little bit, please?

(*The house lights lower.*)

Thanks.

You've got a second to adjust your position in your seat.

Look for something in your bag.

Thank whomever you came with for coming with you.

If it was your idea, be extra nice.

If you're here alone, that's awesome. Thanks for being here.

Okay. Time's up. It's the moment to turn off your phone.

If that makes you nervous, you can just turn the sound off.

But I'd recommend turning it all the way off.

Sometimes, I just like knowing it's all the way off.

We are going straight through the play, which is about ninety minutes long, so hopefully, you had a chance to do whatever you needed to do.

Okay.

Could we take these lights down a tiny bit more, please?

(*The house lights go out.*)

MAPS.   Great. We're ready.

It's [insert day of the week], we're at [insert theater], so thanks again for being here with us. It's a not-for-profit organization [if true], so extra thanks if you've given them money.

Okay. It's [insert time], and we're starting *The Best We Could (a family tragedy)*.

    (The actors are introduced.)

This is Ella.

She grew up dancing ballet, but when she realized she didn't have a future in it, she quit.

She went to college, studied philosophy and studio art, got a job leading museum tours and managing a gift shop, but when she realized she didn't have a future in that either, she quit.

She joined a touring modern dance company, but when they realized their choreographer had been groping teenage boys for decades, they all quit.

Now she teaches chair yoga at a rehab facility in Los Angeles.

She's working on an illustrated book about giving up on your dreams.

This is Ella's mother, Peg.

Peg's a retired event planner. She did private parties and some occasional corporate events, but mostly, weddings. She lives in New Jersey with her husband, Lou.

This is Ella's father, Lou.

Lou was a senior investigator at a biomedical research institute specializing in the study of viral oncogenes, which are as scary as they sound.

This is Marc.

Marc and Lou met in their twenties while they were getting graduate degrees in microbiology.

He and his wife live outside of Denver.

Marc... You're not really in the first part... Sorry to make you wait.

MARC. That's okay.

MAPS. Okay. Ella.

Arrive at a restaurant that serves very small dishes made to share.

It's your birthday. Happy Birthday.

They won't seat you alone, so wait for your girlfriend Crystal at the bar.

Wait thirty minutes. Wait an hour. Leave alone.

Write in your journal: "Carelessness is cruelty. I am in love with someone who will destroy me."

Crystal got caught up in a tarot reading at her hairdresser's bungalow.

She's very sorry. And a little drunk. Again.

Tell Crystal it's over.

Your mother is calling. Answer the phone.

> (**ELLA** *is far away from her parents on the stage.*)

PEG. Are you sitting down?

ELLA. What? What's wrong?

PEG. Are you sitting down?

ELLA. What's wrong?

PEG. Maybe you should sit down.

ELLA. Oh god. What happened?

PEG. ...Is Crystal there with you?

ELLA. No.

PEG. Is anybody else there with you?

ELLA. ...Who else would be here with me?

PEG. ...A friend...or somebody?

ELLA. No.

PEG. Maybe you should sit down.

ELLA. Oh god. What happened?

PEG. Maybe you should sit down.

ELLA. No. Really. What happened?

PEG. You should sit down.

ELLA. I can't do this. What happened?

PEG. Just sit down.

(**ELLA** *is certain that her father is dead.*)

ELLA. I can't sit down... I can't breathe. Mom.

PEG. I'm so sorry. Why don't you just sit down.

ELLA. I'm not doing it. You can't tell me anything horrible because I'm not sitting down.

PEG. I'm so sorry.

ELLA. I'm never sitting down. Please. Mom. I can't take it. I'm so far away.

PEG. Sweetie. I'm so sorry.

ELLA. I can't. Mom. I can't. I can't.

PEG. Sweetie.

ELLA. I can't.

PEG. Sweetie...Brandy died tonight.

ELLA. ...

PEG. I know. I can't even believe it. Barbara was dropping me off after knitting. She parked for a second, because she wanted to see – Brandy. She loves him. She loves to give him a liver treat. So, I opened the side door, and he goes running down the driveway – And we're yelling for him – because it's dark. You know? Finally – He comes wobbling back up to the house, panting. He couldn't catch his breath. He just collapsed. God. It was horrible. ...Are you there?

ELLA. Fuck.

PEG. I know.

ELLA. No. Fuck you, Mom!

PEG. Jesus, Ella!

ELLA. I thought... Fuck!

PEG. Jesus, Ella.

ELLA. I THOUGHT DAD DIED, MOM!

PEG. Jesus, Ella. What is wrong with you?

ELLA. You can't call me and say ARE YOU SITTING DOWN?!

PEG. Jesus Christ. There is something seriously wrong with you.

ELLA. YOU KNOW WHAT "ARE YOU SITTING DOWN" MEANS!

PEG. THE DOG DIED IN MY ARMS, ELLA.

ELLA. I THOUGHT DAD DIED IN YOUR ARMS, MOM!

PEG. Your father is devastated.

ELLA. I feel dizzy.

PEG. Maybe you should sit down.

ELLA. Yeah. I'm gonna sit down...

PEG. Take a breath... Are you okay?

ELLA. Yeah. I'm okay.

PEG. Good.

ELLA. ...I'm okay.

PEG. Well. We are devastated.

ELLA. I'm sorry.

PEG. We rushed him downtown because they have that animal emergency room but... He had his head in my lap. WHEN HE DIED, ELLA.

ELLA. I'm sorry. That's horrible.

PEG. Your father is crying.

ELLA. Oh god.

PEG. He loved that dog.

ELLA. I know.

PEG. It's horrible.

ELLA. I know.

PEG. Do you want to talk to him?

ELLA. Um. I don't know. Does he want to talk to me...?

LOU. ...Elle?

(**ELLA** *is relieved to hear her dad's voice.*)

ELLA. ...Hi, Daddy! I'm so so sorry...about Brandy.

LOU. ...I loved that dog, Elle.

ELLA. I know, Dad. I know. But, you're going to rescue a new dog, and it's going to be a blessing. Right? You're not going to wait three years like you did when Ginger died? Right? I'll help you. We'll do it together. Right?

LOU. Right.

ELLA. I love you, Daddy. I love you so much. I'm so sorry I'm so far away.

LOU. Me too. I love you. Here's Mom.

PEG. ...Hi.

ELLA. Hi.

PEG. Well. Now you see what we're dealing with over here.

MAPS. Lou, fly to California. Get in your daughter's car, and begin a drive across the country to pick up your new dog and deliver him safely home. For now, keep the conversation light and positive.

LOU. This is kind of pretty around here... Sort of... What's that smell?

ELLA. It's the tar pit.

LOU. That's cool.

ELLA. I guess it is kind of cool.

LOU. I'm sweating a little bit.

ELLA. It doesn't go any lower than sixty-two.

LOU. I'll be fine.

ELLA. Is the vent open on your side?

LOU. It's okay. I'll be fine.

ELLA. Have some water.

LOU. Just a little, or I'll have to pee.

MAPS. Rediscover each other and the country that you live in.

ELLA. I have to get a night guard for my teeth.

LOU. Huh. Why?

ELLA. They said I'm clenching my jaw in my sleep, and it's smashing my teeth down to nothing.

LOU. That's weird. I wonder why you do that.

(*He looks at his daughter for a moment – recognizing something he can't put his finger on.*)

Oh hey, can I have the nuts?

MAPS. Offer some valuable wisdom.

LOU. You know what? It's pretty simple. The thing about mortgages is – the first many years, you're not paying your mortgage down at all. It's all interest. But, the interest is tax-deductible.

ELLA. Right.

LOU. So, some people who get mortgages don't even need them. Do you understand?

ELLA. That part – no. Not really.

LOU. Basically, we haven't started paying the mortgage part at all.

ELLA. You could move and rent something smaller, right?

LOU. My parents, they never owned their house. It's been. It's been very important to me that I did that.

ELLA. It's not something I really think about. It doesn't seem feasible. But, also, every three years, I start to hate wherever I am anyway.

LOU. You should think about it.

ELLA. Yeah. I don't, really.

MAPS. Offer more wisdom.

LOU. You know what? It's pretty simple. One way to do it is: they advertise the job, and you write to them and apply. Another way to do it is: they advertise, and then you have your friends send in your resume, and then, when they've seen your resume from three or four very high-level people, then, they call you and ask you to apply for the job. That's the good way to do it.

ELLA. It's all about who you know, right?

LOU. Yeah. Who said that?

ELLA. I don't think anybody "said that."

LOU. I think I said that.

ELLA. Are you thirsty? I'm a little thirsty.

LOU. I'm a little thirsty too. But the really great thing is that I have friends all over the country. I just have to pick up the phone and call them.

MAPS. Go ahead, Peg.

PEG. You always have an excuse!

LOU. You act like I sit here all day twiddling my thumbs.

PEG. I'm done nagging you.

LOU. What are you doing right now?

PEG. I'm done nagging you.

LOU. It doesn't help to nag me on a Saturday.

PEG. I'm done nagging you.

LOU. Nag me during the week between the hours of nine and five when it's appropriate to pick up the phone and call someone.

PEG. I'm done nagging you.

LOU. Good.

PEG. You just say you're going to do something, and then you don't do it.

LOU. Stop nagging me.

PEG. "I have friends all over the country. I just have to pick up the phone and call them."

LOU. Stop nagging me. I'll call Marc on Monday.

PEG. Do what you want. I'm done nagging you.

LOU. I've got so much stuff to do on Monday.

PEG. You're like a broken record. You're like *Groundhog Day*. You've had "so much stuff to do on Monday" for thirty-seven years.

LOU. Stop nagging me.

PEG. *(Switching gears.)* I don't know what happened. I really cooked this salmon. I guess it's on the raw side.

LOU. It tastes a little different.

PEG. I think it will be fine. You want something for dessert?

LOU. I'd have a bite of something.

PEG. I think it's just applesauce.

LOU. ...What's that...exhibit called?

PEG. *Masterpieces and Frauds*. They have, like, masterpieces next to...frauds. I don't know. It might be kind of a waste, but it's something to do.

MAPS. Okay. That's great. Thanks.

Ella and Lou, go four hours out of your way to have lunch at the rim of the Grand Canyon. It might be kind of a waste, but it's something to do.

LOU. You know what? Schlepping to see the pyramids was kind of a waste. The pyramids looked like, sort of just like...slabs. This is better than the pyramids. This is like – wow. I mean – you see what people mean when they talk about this. Come over and see this.

ELLA. I'm good. I'm good right here. I see it. Yeah. It's huge. It's a huge – hole.

LOU. Are you okay?

ELLA. I feel overwhelmed.

LOU. You're okay. We're not hiking or anything. We're just looking at it.

ELLA. It's a very big hole.

LOU. Yeah. Spectacular. Right? It is a very big hole.

ELLA. This very big hole is making me feel very overwhelmed.

LOU. Hold my hand if you need to.

ELLA. I'm okay.

LOU. I won't let you fall in.

ELLA. It doesn't make you feel dizzy?

LOU. Dizzy? No. It's spectacular.

ELLA. I might need to sit down.

LOU. You weren't sure about this – but you've got to admit, you're glad we came.

ELLA. Yeah. Of course. I'm glad I saw it. I'm terrified of it. But I'm glad I saw it.

LOU. Some people climb down there with donkeys and stuff.

ELLA. What?

LOU. Yeah. They do.

ELLA. Crystal and I were supposed to come out here – but from the other side, the Arizona side.

LOU. This is the better side.

ELLA. But she was full of shit, and it probably wasn't even a real plan.

    (A pause.)

LOU. You know what? In some ways, it's better that you're here with me. If you weren't with me, if you were with Crystal or anybody, you'd have to pay at every single park, like a lot of money, but with this senior pass, we've got lifetime access to every single park in the country for ten dollars. It's pretty unbelievable how cheap it is.

ELLA. Maybe they don't think you'll use it too many times.

LOU. Hey, do you want some of my chips? I've got a lot of stuff here.

MAPS. Notice a lady with a nice-looking dog with a big fluffy head and a bright pink tongue.

LOU. *(To* **ELLA***.)* What kind of dog is that?

ELLA. Maybe a Collie?

MAPS. I'll play this lady with the dog.

LOU. WHAT KIND OF DOG IS THAT?

LADY WITH THE DOG. Awww. He's a Miniature Australian Shepherd.

LOU. Wow. Miniature Australian Shepherd! Beautiful dog, very well behaved.

LADY WITH THE DOG. Awww. They're a smart breed.

LOU. How old is he?

LADY WITH THE DOG. Awww! He's my baby. He's four. I had two, but my other one passed away in June.

LOU. Our dog died in June.

LADY WITH THE DOG. Awww! June this year?

LOU. June this year. With our last dog, we waited three years, and it was just too long to wait.

LADY WITH THE DOG. Awww. I know. The love you get from them is just –

LOU.	**LADY WITH THE DOG**.
It's incredible.	It's incredible.

LADY WITH THE DOG. Awww.

LOU. That's actually why we're here.

LADY WITH THE DOG. Awww. You want to scatter your dead dog's ashes at the Grand Canyon.

ELLA. Actually, no.

LOU. You know what? It's pretty interesting. We found this new dog through this organization – and usually, this organization, they don't do out-of-state adoptions, but I wrote to this woman who runs this place, and I explained my situation...how my dog just all of a sudden got this condition where he couldn't breathe properly... It's called –

LOU.	**LADY WITH THE DOG**.
Laryngeal Paralysis	Laryngeal Paralysis

LADY WITH THE DOG. Awww. Mine too.

LOU. Is that a coincidence, or what?

LADY WITH THE DOG. Awww. What a sad coincidence.

LOU. You know what? Our new dog – he's a rescue dog, but he's a pure breed because, well...one of his grandmothers was in the Westminster Dog Show...his previous owners wanted a hunting dog, but this dog wouldn't hunt.

LADY WITH THE DOG. Awww. The doggie wouldn't hunt.

LOU. Our old dog, Brandy, he used to jump into bed with me in the morning and lick my face and... I knew it wasn't my wife because I could feel the whiskers!

LADY WITH THE DOG. *(To* **ELLA**.*)* Awww. You definitely don't have whiskers.

ELLA. Actually, this is my dad.

LADY WITH THE DOG. Awww. You're spending special time with your dad before you go to college.

ELLA. Actually, I'm thirty-six.

LADY WITH THE DOG. Awww. Dogs just bring you so much joy.

LOU. We've got to get your e-mail or something!

LADY WITH THE DOG. Awww? ...For what?

LOU. We'll send you a picture!

LADY WITH THE DOG. Oh. Awww... I don't know. Send it to Dog Lovers Anonymous or something.

ELLA. Do you want some ice cream?

LOU. Yeah, get something, and I'll have a bite.

LADY WITH THE DOG. Awww. Get the apple pie. It's really the best apple pie.

(**LADY WITH THE DOG** *goes.*)

LOU. See, wherever I go, I end up talking to people.

ELLA. Yeah. Whether they like it or not.

LOU. Hey! She was very friendly. And talk about a coincidence!

ELLA. We should get a snow globe while we're here.

LOU. Right on, baby!

MAPS. Gently remind your daughter that most of her eggs are gone for good.

LOU. You know what? It's pretty simple.

ELLA. Actually, it's pretty complicated.

LOU. And, you know what? You've got to have some sperm.

ELLA. No kidding. Really?

LOU. Really! You know, no matter who your partner is –

ELLA. Okay. Let's just –

LOU. No matter if you're with a man, or if it's a woman, or, you know, somebody in-between.

ELLA. Wow. Please stop.

LOU. The reality is: you've got to have some sperm.

ELLA. I don't even have a partner. I don't even have a dishwasher. I've got things on my list ahead of sperm.

LOU. You want to have kids, don't you?

ELLA. I don't know. I'll think about it.

LOU. You'll think about it? You don't have all that much time.

ELLA. Thanks. But. It's a huge decision.

LOU. It's not really.

ELLA. I just don't know. At some point, I'd consider maybe trying to have one or adopting one.

LOU. You know what? It's better to have two, I think.

ELLA. You have to know why you're doing it. I think. You have to know why you do anything.

LOU. Why?

ELLA. Never mind the fact that I'm not really set up to support another human life – I just don't know if I feel totally comfortable having any kids at all unless I'm convinced that we're on a better path…as a species.

LOU. What's that great thing somebody famous said? "…The moral arc of the universe is long, and it bends toward justice."

ELLA. I've also heard it bends toward chaos.

LOU. No. But I think I'm right. Yeah. There are problems. But. You know. There have been problems, like big problems, since in the beginning of time. And that hasn't stopped people.

ELLA. The fact that we're even in this situation right now is so massively fucked up and kind of your fault.

LOU. My fault?

ELLA. Not you specifically. The greater: "you."

LOU. Well. It's not *my* fault. And you know what? Maybe your kid is the person who figures it out.

ELLA. Yeah. I'm pretty sure that's not gonna happen.

LOU. Maybe you should just put it in your calendar to really think about it. And just write out all the steps. Just for example, like: Step one: A more professional job with better benefits. Step two: Marriage to a person you love. Step three: Baby.

ELLA. You forgot the sperm.

LOU. The sad thing about my dad being so old is that he didn't meet you. I want to meet your children. I want to be able to give them things.

PEG. Who can keep track of all these things?

MAPS. Go ahead, Peg.

PEG. It's too much crap! We don't have any more savings to pay the taxes! I am getting rid of this house!

LOU. What's that have to do with anything?

PEG. Stop pestering me! I made a mistake! Who cares! You don't make mistakes? You haven't made any mistakes in your life?

LOU. I've never thrown somebody's childhood memories in the garbage without asking if they wanted to keep anything.

PEG. I am still getting dressed in here. I cannot stand you crowding around me. Monopolizing everything.

LOU. You didn't talk to her – she's very upset.

PEG. I understand she's upset. But. Give me a break.

LOU. She's devastated.

PEG. Oh, she's devastated? Well, she'll have to get over it.

LOU. I know exactly the box she's talking about.

PEG. If it was so important to her, you'd think she would have mentioned it in the last fifteen years. Like, "Oh, where is that box with that stuff from my childhood? I want to take a look at it and see what's in there."

LOU. It's not stuff she wants now; it's stuff she wants to give to her children.

PEG. Okay. First of all – She doesn't have children.

LOU. Maybe someday, she will have children.

PEG. Okay. Well, maybe someday, when she has children, she'll realize that all this shit – is just crap!

LOU. Maybe someday, when she has children, she'll be sad that she has nothing to give them.

PEG. Okay. Well. Maybe someday, when she has children, she can give them your three-hundred-piece snow globe collection. How much shit can you have? She's not even married. She doesn't even have a dishwasher. I don't think she's having children.

LOU. Apologize to your daughter.

PEG. The two of you are ridiculous. I am throwing this shit away, and I am selling this house.

LOU. And where are we going to go?

PEG. That's another problem!

LOU. You know what? It's pretty simple. From now on, there is not a single thing in this house that I can live without.

PEG. You live on another planet.

LOU. DON'T TOUCH A SINGLE TINY THING.

PEG. Don't you yell at me. You have to face reality. This realtor woman looked in the closet, and I was humiliated.

LOU. WHAT ABOUT ALL YOUR SHIT FROM YOUR MOTHER'S HOUSE?

PEG. MY BROTHER STOLE ALL MY SHIT FROM MY MOTHER'S HOUSE.

LOU. GET RID OF ALL THE PICTURES OF THAT STUPID LAKE.

PEG. I'LL GET RID OF EVERY PICTURE OF THAT STUPID LAKE, IF YOU GET RID OF ALL YOUR FUCKING PLAQUES.

LOU. THE FUCKING PLAQUES ARE MEANT TO HANG ON THE WALL OF AN OFFICE.

PEG. WHAT OFFICE?

LOU. MY NEW OFFICE SOMEWHERE.

PEG. YOU DON'T HAVE A NEW OFFICE SOMEWHERE.

LOU. I WILL HAVE A NEW OFFICE SOMEWHERE!

PEG. YOU'RE NOT GOING TO HAVE ANY NEW OFFICE ANYWHERE! YOU'RE OLD AND NOBODY WILL HIRE YOU.

MAPS. That's enough. Thanks. Look forward toward a happier future.

LOU. You know what? Somebody once said:

(*He chuckles.*)

Actually, it might have been me.

"It's not about what you have, but who you're having it with." Maybe you're right. Maybe we don't really need a whole house. We could get a little apartment somewhere nice. Maybe in Boston.

ELLA. Boston?

LOU. Boston is phenomenal.

ELLA. Nobody thinks that about Boston.

LOU. I don't think you've ever really spent much time in Boston. Oh! This is Copper Mountain, Colorado!

ELLA. I think we missed Aspen.

LOU. Yeah, but this is Copper Mountain, Colorado!

ELLA. I sort of wanted to know – What is Aspen?

LOU. It's a ski town in Colorado.

ELLA. I know. Crystal's family couldn't believe I'd never been to Aspen.

LOU. I had the best week of my life in Copper Mountain, Colorado.

ELLA. Crystal's sister named her daughter Aspen, which I actually thought was really tacky.

LOU. Do you remember my friend Gordon?

ELLA. Gordon who?

LOU. Gordon Bombardo!

ELLA. Nope.

LOU. Gordon was a year older than me, and his brother was a year younger than me, and his brother and I went to summer camp together. So, we were all – kind of good friends. Gordon's cousin runs the education program at the Holocaust museum, and he played basketball for Cornell, which was a big deal at the time. This other guy Len Antonoff, who had been a piano student of your grandmother's, he went to Copper Mountain with this other guy, Rick Segal, and this other guy Wolf Williams, whose father was my dentist, and he told Gordon about it, and Gordon told me, I told my friend Marc, and then Gordon sold an antique clock, and then Gordon, Marc and I all went to Copper Mountain. They even made a movie about it.

ELLA. Actually, I don't care about Aspen at all.

LOU. They had these really nice, comfortable benches, and I fell asleep in the middle of the cocktail party on the first night. It was really funny. Everybody was like, who is this guy? How can he be so cool to sleep through the cocktail party at The Club Med Copper Mountain? I had the best time. I met all these cool people.

MARC. I just met all these cool people.

MAPS. It's 1978 – the second cocktail party at the Club Med Copper Mountain.

LOU. Yeah. This is great. I don't even need to ski. I can have a great time right here in the lodge.

MARC. You can't see what anyone looks like when they're skiing anyway.

LOU. Exactly. I say we get as much rest as possible during the day and save our energy for this.

MARC. Yeah. But, no. I have to try to ski at least a few times if we came all the way out here.

LOU. ...You might be too busy.

MARC. ...Nah. She's been commandeered by the guy who flies helicopters.

LOU. I might have done you a huge favor while you were at the bar getting us drinks.

MARC. Did you talk to her? What did you say? What did she say?

LOU. She's very interested...

MARC. For real?

LOU. Yeah. I talked you way up!

MARC. For real?

LOU. I told her I wouldn't be here without you. ...Because you saved my life.

MARC. ...I what?

LOU. I didn't get into specifics. I said you're very humble, but it's a great story, and you'd probably tell it if she lets you buy her a drink.

MARC. Why couldn't you just tell her I'm super rich or something?

LOU. This will work much better. I promise. It's going to be great. You don't even need to say anything. She's pretty loaded already. It's not going to matter one bit. Just ask her if she wants to see the view from our room.

MARC. Our room looks over the parking lot.

LOU. So? It's a view! You miss one hundred percent of the shots you don't take. My father always used to say that. With one more drink in her, I think this bullseye might be hard to miss.

MARC. You're right. ...Maybe I've got a decent shot.

LOU. I'm rooting for you.

MARC. Thanks. I'm rooting for me too.

ELLA. Forget Aspen. Colorado is beautiful, but I don't need to see Aspen.

MAPS. Try to offer some more wisdom.

LOU. You know what? It's pretty simple. You can get real sophisticated about it. But, at the end of the day, there are only two things to invest in: stocks and bonds. Okay?

ELLA. Okay.

LOU. So. Bonds and stocks tend to move in opposite directions. Okay?

ELLA. Okay. But investing for retirement isn't really relevant when I'm still paying off loans from a useless college degree.

LOU. Come on. You're glad you went to college.

ELLA. Am I? I don't know if that's true.

LOU. Of course, you're glad you went to college. You were Phi Beta Kappa!

ELLA. Nobody cares about that.

LOU. People do care about that.

ELLA. No. They really don't.

LOU. But it's on your resume, right?

ELLA. I'm a yoga teacher. I don't really have a resume.

LOU. You're not just a yoga teacher. You wrote a book!

ELLA. It's just a fun thing. It was more of a hobby.

LOU. And you said some of these yoga people make a lot of money.

ELLA. Yeah. I'm not that kind of yoga person.

LOU. But when your book comes out, maybe you can quit your day job, right? Isn't that what they say when someone has a big hit? "You can quit your day job?"

ELLA. It's not really a day job. It's just a regular job.

LOU. But, it's not like a long-term kind of career job.

(A pause.)

ELLA. I don't know. Maybe it is. For me. ...Remind me again, what are their kids' names?

LOU. Patrick, Paul...and Pierre. When you were little, we all went to Atlantic City, and you let Pierre cut your hair in the bathroom.

ELLA. ...Oh yeah... Why'd they name him Pierre?

LOU. Marc's wife became sort of a real... Like a Francophile. She's not from France or anything.

MAPS. At a steak chain in Denver, rendezvous with Marc, who was very happy to hear from you when you called, and his wife Karen. Karen is from Orlando, but she speaks with a heavy French accent. I'll do my best with that.

(A restaurant in Denver. **KAREN** *and* **MARC** *are there.* **KAREN** *has a French accent.)*

LOU. His previous owners wanted a hunting dog, but this dog wouldn't hunt.

KAREN. Oh, là là! How bizarre! The doggie would not hunt.

MARC. I tell you, these trips with your kid are wonderful. I treasure every one of them.

ELLA. Are you treasuring it, Dad?

LOU. Oh, I'm treasuring it. We're hitting Mt. Rushmore tomorrow. I've always wanted to see that.

KAREN. Ah oui. See it now before they take it away.

MARC. I don't think it's going anywhere.

KAREN. The Indians don't want this big statue of these White men's faces on their land. They have come to resent it, I think.

ELLA. Isn't it built on sacred land that was stolen from Indigenous tribes?

MARC. Maybe so. Maybe so.

ELLA. It's not really a maybe.

(An uncomfortable pause.)

...So, how long have you two known each other?

MARC. I felt so bad for your dad. He shows up – walking around in a blue oxford and khaki shorts. Khaki shorts! Nobody wore khaki shorts! And I'm thinking, "Where is this guy from?"

LOU. I went out and bought a pair of cowboy boots, and I was so proud of them, and I walked to the front of the class, and I put my feet up, and I said: Look at that! I finally got a pair of José Mamas! And everybody laughed.

ELLA. Why did they laugh?

MARC. 'Cause, it's Tony Lamas, not José Mamas.

KAREN. It is very hard to be alone in a new place.

MARC. I felt so bad for this poor guy.

MAPS. It's 1982. A different chain restaurant.

MARC. He shows up, walking around in a blue oxford and khaki shorts. Khaki shorts! Nobody wore khaki shorts!

LOU. What are you guys doing for the holidays?

KAREN. We're actually going to Paris! I'm so excited. In high school, I got very into wearing berets and eating soft cheese.

LOU. I hate to talk shop at the dinner table, but I finally cornered Bruce Cho.

MARC. And?

LOU. He says it's the best paper ever to come out of this lab.

MARC. You called it!

(They high-five. It's nerdy.)

LOU. He thinks *The Journal* will be very interested.

MARC. Holy shit.

LOU. Bladder Carcinoma Transformation for the win!

MARC. Holy shit.

LOU. I'm making a plug for you as first author.

MARC. Wow... Okay.

LOU. I was on a great paper last year. This is your moment.

MARC. I think you're drunk. But I'm holding you to this!

LOU. I may be drunk, but I'm completely sober.

MARC. Let's get another bottle!

(The scene shifts back to the present.)

ELLA. Probably not for us. We have to be on the road early tomorrow. Right?

LOU. Ella has an important meeting in New York. So, this really worked out.

KAREN. Oh bravo! Bravo.

LOU. She wrote a book!

MARC. You wrote a book!

ELLA. It's – An illustrated book.

LOU. It's really neat!

MARC. Look at that, man! Your kid wrote a book!

KAREN. I love to read. I read three books every year.

ELLA. ...That's wonderful.

KAREN. Tell us what your book is about!

ELLA. Oh. Well. It's sort of about the inner emptiness of being a person living in a war-like society that, on some level, believes it has no future. And how we find it harder and harder to establish a connection with the world around us. And how we demand way too much of our lives and way too little of ourselves. And how the modern consumerist culture has us swinging between this, sort of incredible entitlement and panicky, miserable dissatisfaction. And how we look to others to validate our sense of self. And our bottomless need to be admired for power-coded characteristics that ultimately fade with time. And how we are unable to achieve any kind of lasting satisfaction in the form of love and meaningful care. And how basically, the only way to be happy is to just renounce the right to be happy.

KAREN. Bravo.

MARC. And it's for kids?

ELLA. Yeah. It's more fun than it sounds. One of the characters is a sheep.

MARC. Sounds very creative.

LOU. She's very talented.

MARC. Talented and beautiful!

KAREN. Such a pretty girl.

ELLA. That makes me kind of uncomfortable... But. I'm just going to eat an asparagus.

KAREN. I love having after dinner...you know...cappuccino or latte. But last time I did that, I could not sleep.

LOU. So. I heard that Greg O'Conner left?

MARC. Yeah. I think they're moving to Arizona.

LOU. So, what's going on with Greg's job?

MARC. You wouldn't want Greg's job, right? It's not really a higher-level thing.

LOU. I don't really need a higher-level thing.

KAREN. The crust is...! You have to have that, Marco. The crust is...parfait.

MARC. It looks more like pie than parfait.

LOU. So, maybe you could put my name forward? For Greg's job?

MARC. Really?

LOU. Well. Yeah.

MARC. Sure! Yeah! But you'll still have to go through with all the formal search committee stuff.

LOU. I don't mind all that. You know me. I can really talk to anybody. Who's heading up the committee? Would I know the person?

MARC. Well. We're in luck there because it's me!

LOU. No kidding!

KAREN. What a...coincidence!

ELLA. Look at that, Dad!

LOU. Yeah. Look at that! You know, I was sort of surprised that Greg was leaving right now. I just saw his name on a big paper.

MARC. You didn't hear it from me. But... He was writing love letters to a doctoral candidate.

LOU. No kidding.

MARC. She kept telling him no and telling him no. And he kept writing better letters and better letters.

LOU. Well, at least the letters got better.

KAREN. This oppressive infantilization of young women is very dangerous. It is not a crime to seduce someone, even if you're doing it badly...

ELLA. But, actually, this sounds like, this is like – stalking. At work.

KAREN. I just don't think a woman should be running to a committee every time something goes wrong on a date. I really oppose that kind of thing.

ELLA. I actually really oppose harassment and intimidation of any kind.

LOU. It does seem like Greg went sort of off the deep end.

MARC. You should have seen some of these letters...

LOU. Oh, I'd love to! Maybe you can show me later.

ELLA. Dad. Come on. It's not funny.

KAREN. These puritanical rules against personal freedoms – that does not seem like égalité to me.

ELLA. That's exactly the thing men have said throughout history to keep things the way they are.

KAREN. Women are so vulnerable now. You can't say anything at all, or we scream victimhood.

ELLA. I think I should go.

KAREN. Oh, I have offended. Je suis désolé.

LOU. You're not going anywhere. She's a little sensitive.

MARC. It's alright. It's possible we're a little out of touch with the latest fashions.

KAREN. Tell her about Benjamin.

MARC. Our little nephew Benjamin has a cabaret show and is also a bisexual.

ELLA. I think I should just wait for you in the car.

KAREN. Ma chérie. You have to understand. The real world outside your daddy's house is much harsher than you are willing to believe.

ELLA. OKAY. SO, YOU ARE ABOUT AS FRENCH AS MY SIDE ORDER OF FRIES, SO, HOW ABOUT YOU DROP THE FAKE FUCKING ACCENT YOU HATEFUL FUCKING BITCH!

PEG. Jesus, Ella.

MAPS. Back in the car, apologize to your parents for being rude to their friends.

(*A phone call with* **PEG**.)

ELLA. I'm sorry. But, she's a mean fucking cunt.

PEG. Jesus, Ella!

LOU. We'd had a long day. Maybe we were dehydrated.

ELLA. I'll throw French fries in that cunt's face again. Anytime.

PEG. Jesus, Ella.

LOU. They were very understanding. It's fine. When you've known somebody as long as we have...it just has to be fine.

PEG. How was the house?

ELLA. It was gross.

LOU. Oh, it was really nice. Huge. Too. And they have a tiny horse! I got a picture with the tiny horse!

PEG. Sounds nice.

ELLA. Why do they have a tiny horse?

PEG. Sounds nice.

ELLA. It's cruel to ride a tiny horse if you're not a tiny person.

PEG. Take me off the speaker.

LOU. Okay. I'll take you off the speaker.

PEG. Did you get to talk to Marc?

LOU. We did. We talked about a lot of stuff.

PEG. Is he going to make sure you're on the top of the pile for Greg's job?

LOU. Yup. He'll make sure.

PEG. That's good news. Right?

LOU. Absolutely. As long as you like Denver.

PEG. For some reason, my computer is pulling up all my old photos and using it as a screensaver. It doesn't really bother me, but I didn't program it to do that. Do you know how to fix it?

ELLA. It's not something I have the patience to explain over the phone.

PEG. Am I still on the speaker? Jesus, Lou. Whatever. Elle, don't ask me how I know this, but Crystal's parents moved to New Hampshire somewhere. They bought a log house with a pool, I guess. I've never heard of anything like that. Do you know what kind of house they bought?

ELLA. Nope.

PEG. It's so isolated. I guess they stayed together, though, huh? Are you still on good terms with her?

ELLA. No. Not really.

PEG. Well. I'd just be curious to know about that house. I'd just like to know what it looks like on the inside and how much they paid for it.

MAPS. Marvel at the spectacle of Mount Rushmore. A four-headed sarcophagus – etched in the image of four dead men who did more than four terrible things. It wasn't supposed to be just the heads. They were supposed to have torsos, but they ran out of money.

ELLA. ...Well. There it is.

LOU. Wow! There it is! Yeah. Look at that! You know, I always wanted to see that.

ELLA. I'm kind of confused.

LOU. Don't you see the four faces?

ELLA. Yeah. I do. But am I supposed to feel like this is a great country because we did a mediocre job carving these creepy faces on a beautiful mountain? Putting aside the fact that two of these guys owned slaves – It's just, like, not a great piece of public art. The spacing is pretty wonky. Teddy Roosevelt seems like he's being sucked into a vortex. Lincoln only has half a beard. I'm supposed to feel moved? I feel haunted. It's kind of absolutely chilling. It's also kind of chilly.

LOU. Do you want my sweater?

ELLA. I'm okay.

LOU. We don't have to stay long. I've seen it now. It's sort of like I thought it would be. ...Maybe I thought it would be a little bigger. But, hey, I bet they have a lot of snow globes here.

MAPS. Explain your theory about the Kennedy assassination.

LOU. You know what? It's pretty simple. There had to be a visual signal that it was still on, and so, the opening of the umbrella, because it was right in line with the bullet, that was the signal for it to happen. What do you need?

ELLA. I thought I had some pretzels.

LOU. I'm sorry. I think I ate them. I thought they were my pretzels.

ELLA. Don't be sorry! They were our pretzels. We can stop and get some more. Except. I'm not sure where... This has to be the Badlands.

LOU. Wow. Yeah, it has to be.

ELLA. If I was naming this place, I'd definitely say, ooh, that's bad.

LOU. Good times in the Badlands. Ha-ha.

ELLA. Ha-ha.

LOU. The guide said the Lakota tribe called it "mako-sica" and because the land is so barren, they had to compete for food with the grizzly bears and the coyote, who were also trying to eat the bison.

ELLA. I'd probably just let the bear eat me. I don't have any of that survival of the fittest competitive drive type of thing.

LOU. Well, of course, you do.

ELLA. Like, I could teach at one of those studios where the classes are fifty bucks a pop, and they spray you with liquid gold in savasana or whatever.

LOU. I don't know what that means, but it sounds like a step in the right direction.

ELLA. I'm good at the rehab center. I'm teaching people that really need help. And giving them tools that should be free in the first place. I realized something a couple years ago. Crystal and I went to a tea ceremony called The Vine of Death –

LOU. The what?

ELLA. The Vine of Death. Which is a good name for it because after I vomited up my life, I *did* see my own death, and it *was* like a grape hanging on a vine.

LOU. Jesus. You were vomiting like that?

ELLA. Yeah. But seeing my own death on The Vine of Death was very clarifying. I realized that I'm not interested in doing anything that's...really competitive.

LOU. If you were vomiting like that, you should have called us!

ELLA. I don't have to always be striving towards the next thing.

LOU. You have to want things. Otherwise, what's the point of doing anything at all?

ELLA. I don't know exactly... Maybe, being of service...?

LOU. Yeah, but that's not how the world works. That's not how we kept you in ballet lessons and piano lessons, and whatever you wanted from the mall, and a math tutor when you needed one, and special twelve dollar peanut butter when you decided whatever oil was poisonous, and that's not how you got the very car you drive today. Right now, you're young and healthy, but one day you won't be, and you'll want a safety net.

ELLA. I'm not trying to say I have everything figured out.

LOU. But, the great thing is: you're very talented, and you're very creative, and you made a very beautiful book that lots of people will want to buy.

ELLA. I didn't see anything out there for kids debunking the myth that hard work will lead to a better life.

LOU. Well. You're working hard and it's really paying off.

MAPS. Bask in the awesomeness of The Corn Palace of Mitchell, South Dakota.

ELLA. ...I guess the whole thing isn't made of corn.

LOU. That's kind of neat. It's a museum and a high school gym. But where's the corn?

ELLA. Oh! See? That Willie Nelson mural is made of corn!

LOU. Oh hey. That's corn!

ELLA. I thought the whole thing would be made of corn. But maybe that didn't make any sense.

LOU. You know what? I have to pee.

MAPS. Go inside. Buy your dad a snow globe in the gift shop. Surprise him with it over dinner at a rest stop. He's so happy about this stupid little thing. Ask him about the death of his father. Ask him about marrying your mother. Ask him about the house they lived in when you were born. Try to remember the stories. The point of doing anything at all might be in there.

LOU. You know what? You make decisions, and by making those decisions, you learn something.

MARC. I just can't kick myself over every single decision. You know?

MAPS. Marc calls late at night. He's having a couple of drinks. He's out in the barn with his tiny horse, which is where he likes to go when he's having a couple of drinks.

MARC. I'm just out in the barn with my tiny horse. Having a couple of drinks. How'd you feel about the phone interview?

LOU. Look. I just couldn't help it; I finally just said: Hey, can I ask you how old you are?

MARC. Come on! You're not really supposed to ask that. Especially when you're the person being interviewed.

LOU. I couldn't develop any rapport with the woman. It was like she hadn't even read my CV, considered my experience…

(**MARC** *stifles a giggle.*)

What's going on?

MARC. Fondue licked my hand, and it tickles.

LOU. It was kind of disrespectful, the whole interaction. We'd only just started talking and – She said she had a "hard stop" at two o'clock, whatever that means, and then her "hard stop" came, and she rushed me off the phone.

MARC. That sucks. I'm sorry.

LOU. I just feel like someone should talk to this kid and tell her that I am a strong candidate for this job and many different jobs, and that I was sort of upset by this interaction.

MARC. Look. I'll smooth things over. I'll figure out something to say. But it's a really competitive pool of people, and you've just got to play the game a little bit.

LOU. I can play the game. I am playing the game.

MARC. Even if you feel like you're talking to someone who doesn't get it.

LOU. I know you get it.

MARC. I get it. And I'm gonna do everything I can on my end. I'll make some calls this week and drum up some support with some of the folks here that know you. It would be so great if this works out!

LOU. I'd love for us to be all together in Dallas.

MARC. We're in Denver. Right, pretty girl? Fondue and her daddy live in Denver.

LOU. Denver. Dallas. Detroit. Des Moines. Wherever.

MARC. Pee-ew Fondue! Something did not agree with you!

LOU. I've got a good feeling about this.

MAPS. Convince your daughter to find a partner in your image, someone who will keep her safe when you are gone.

LOU. You know what? It's pretty simple. And it's all about basic underpinnings.

ELLA. I mean...there's something to that. I aspire to be the kind of person who has an organized drawer full of basic, very comfortable underpinnings.

PEG. Do you have any good news today?

MAPS. Hang on a second.

LOU. No. I'm talking about ethical, intellectual, basic principles of living. Those kinds of underpinnings. I just mean spirit. Crystal's...spirit... She seemed kind of different to me.

ELLA. Crystal is a toxic narcissist with a drinking problem, So that might be why her spirit seemed kind of different to you.

LOU. Well, you didn't tell me about that part.

PEG. Do you have any good news today?

MAPS. Hang on a second, Peg.

LOU. You have to find someone you can talk to. Your mother and I, we talk about everything. There isn't anything we can't talk about.

PEG. Do you have any good news today?

LOU. *(Turning to* **PEG**.*)* You know what? It's pretty simple. I don't want you to say that to me anymore. If something good happens, you will be the first to know. I will tell you first like I always do. So, if I don't tell you anything, then you should know that nothing good happened today.

PEG. I kind of like these lettuce-wrap things.

LOU. Is that what this is?

PEG. Jill said Roger had to have a feeding tube installed.

LOU. Shit.

PEG. It's the end of solid food for Roger.

LOU. Poor Roger.

PEG. Roger loved these lettuce wrap things. What's your fortune say?

LOU. "Work is the elixir of life. The busiest man is the happiest man."

PEG. Your motto. Tape that to your forehead.

LOU. Right on, baby!

PEG. I don't understand. If your friends in Arkansas did everything they could –

LOU. Scotty said they absolutely loved me.

PEG. Everybody absolutely loves you.

LOU. But, you know, they picked somebody else. Peg. Don't cry. It's gonna be okay.

PEG. What? I'm not crying. Eat your lettuce wrap thing.

LOU. Peggy.

PEG. Do you want any dessert?

LOU. Sure, whatever you like.

PEG. I should put this pie in the freezer. It's not going to keep.

LOU. Keep it out. I'll have a bite.

PEG. I'll put it in foil, and we can see what happens.

MAPS. Walk half a mile to a Kenosha, Wisconsin diner you saw on the Food Network that may or may not be temporarily closed.

ELLA. Snorkeling is one of those words that sounds like what it means. Snork-el-ing. Snork-el-ing. Snork-el-ing.

LOU. If this meeting in New York with the book people goes well – Well, what would be like, the next steps?

ELLA. I'm not really sure.

LOU. They'll publish your book, right?

ELLA. Yeah. I'm not sure.

LOU. Maybe they would give you a big advance.

ELLA. I don't know about that.

LOU. Maybe they would turn your book into a movie.

ELLA. Yeah. I'm not sure.

LOU. Oh yeah! All the best books get turned into a movie.

ELLA. Well. Not always successfully.

LOU. They already think you're very talented.

ELLA. Maybe. I'm not sure.

LOU. Well, of course, they do! Or they wouldn't be inviting you to come all the way to their office for a meeting!

(The past overlaps with the present.)

PEG. Don't say you're not sure.

ELLA. I don't know. I'm not sure.

PEG. He can barely get out of bed, Ella.

ELLA. What do you mean he can barely get out of bed?

PEG. He needs something to look forward to. I do too. I'm just ready for some good news. I'm starting to feel like nothing's ever going to happen. You get depressed. It's depressing. I'd love to see him get something, but Arkansas? Could you imagine? I can't start over in Arkansas. At my age? I'd kill myself. But it's still so depressing that they didn't pick him. He gets an interview, and then they just don't – I don't know what happens. When it comes down to it, they take somebody else... So, Dad will fly to L.A., and you'll drive together in your car to pick up the dog. You told him you'd help him, so you'll help him.

ELLA. I don't know if I can –

PEG. What else do you have to do?

ELLA. I have a job. I have a life. This is like a two-week trip.

PEG. Get someone else to cover for you.

ELLA. I'm the only one who teaches in my specialty.

PEG. Come on, Elle, he really needs you.

ELLA. Okay. Fine. I'll do it.

PEG. Great. I've got it all worked out.

LOU. Did you bring a copy of your resume?

ELLA. No.

LOU. You should probably bring a couple copies of your resume, right?

ELLA. Well. No. I don't think that kind of thing matters.

LOU. You should bring a couple copies of your resume, just in case. I've got some nice paper you can use. You've got your Phi Beta Kappa thing on there, right?

ELLA. Truly no one cares about that.

LOU. You never know what connection you're going to make when you meet someone, what kind of coincidences could become a big opportunity. Why isn't your Phi Beta Kappa thing on there?

ELLA. I don't know.

LOU. You're going to have to speak a few more words than that in the meeting, right? You're going to have to really sell yourself!

ELLA. I don't know. I'm not sure.

PEG. Before Dad gets to L.A. and you guys start driving – I just wanted to call you to mention one tiny thing.

ELLA. I had the oil changed.

PEG. Oh good. That's good.

ELLA. See? You can just trust me to do what I say I'm going to do.

PEG. I just wanted to mention. So. So. I told your father that you had an important meeting with a publisher in New York for your children's book. That you sent us. It's nice. You did a good job with it, Elle. He said it was beautiful and someone should publish it. So, I told him someone wants to publish it...are you there?

ELLA. MOM!

PEG. What?

ELLA. I got a bunch of "no, thank you" letters from those publishers!

PEG. Well. You didn't tell me that!

ELLA. Maybe I wanted to process my rejection in private.

PEG. What did they say?

ELLA. One of them called it an impenetrable and derivative Marxist screed!

PEG. Is that a bad thing?

ELLA. They didn't mean it as a compliment!

PEG. Well. Okay... Maybe we could just keep that between us for right now. He's really excited for you.

ELLA. Mom. This is nuts.

PEG. I begged him to ask you. But he just wouldn't. He didn't want you to have to miss work. They won't fly the new dog. He was going to do the drive alone. And that made me very nervous. Someone who can't get out of bed, crying about how he can't go on.

ELLA. What do you mean he was crying about how he can't go on?

PEG. I'd go with him, but I've really got to stay home. I'm organizing Roger's meal train. I mean, Jill's meal train, you know – Roger can't eat. It's horrible. I can't stand the idea of him driving for hours and hours. Alone. Sometimes, even I look at those lines on the road... You know. When you're alone, you know, and you're really upset, and you're driving? There's a reason they call a car a death machine. So, I told him you need help getting to your meeting because you're afraid to fly. Which is the truth.

ELLA. That is not the truth!

PEG. You were terrified.

ELLA. I was twelve!

PEG. Absolutely terrified.

ELLA. Apologize for lying.

PEG. I'm not apologizing. If you can't tell a white lie to make a man who is suffering feel necessary, then I think you should be ashamed of yourself. I am doing the best I can here, and you don't seem to understand that.

ELLA. I'll deal with it. Just apologize.

PEG. I'm not apologizing.

ELLA. Come on. Just apologize.

PEG. I'm not apologizing. You'll have to get over it. I just tried the new Fresh Market that opened yesterday.

ELLA. Oh, how is it?

PEG. ...Okay. A little disappointing. But what are you going to do?

MAPS. Pull into a long driveway and approach a farmhouse standing alone on a grassy hill. Try to figure out which dog is your dog.

*(Eventually, **LOU** and **ELLA** find their dog.)*

You found him.

ELLA. That's him!

MAPS. Call Peg and tell her how your new dog is, in many ways, a better dog than the one who died.

ELLA. He's got a lot of energy! Brandy was kind of lazy.

PEG. Hey! May he rest in peace!

ELLA. May he rest in peace.

LOU. He jumps right in the car! Brandy was kind of anxious about the car.

PEG. Hey! May he rest in peace.

LOU. May he rest in peace.

ELLA. He puts his paws on you, but in a gentle way, not like Brandy.

PEG.	LOU.	ELLA.
May he rest in peace.	May he rest in peace.	May he rest in peace.

ELLA. His breath isn't nearly as bad as Brandy's.

PEG. Don't let him kiss you on the mouth.

ELLA. Too late.

LOU. Are we okay with...uh... Candy? They told us we could change it if we want to.

PEG. We could get it confused with Brandy.

ELLA. *(Baby-talking to the dog.)* He likes it when I sing to him:

HEY, I JUST PET YOU,
AND YOU ARE CRAZY,
BUT YOU'RE MY FAVORITE,
CANDY BABY!

PEG. They said he's house-trained, right? I just cannot have a dog peeing all over my carpets, Lou. I am selling this house.

LOU. ...He's mostly house-trained.

ELLA. Just like Brandy.

PEG.	LOU.	ELLA.
May he rest in peace.	May he rest in peace.	May he rest in peace.

PEG. ...Brandy had fifteen-hundred dollars worth of dental work just the week before he died.

LOU. Well. You're going to love this dog. This is a very good dog!

PEG. I'm exhausted. I gotta lie down. I just got back from my mammogram.

(A long pause.)

...They said everything's fine.

MAPS. Peg, try a class at the YMCA. Follow the woman in front of you who seems to know what she's doing. I'll be Adele, a Zumba enthusiast originally from Delaware.

PEG. Adele!

(**ADELE** *tries not to engage.*)

Adele!

(**ADELE** *dances.* **PEG** *follows her, not worrying about the steps.*)

Adele! I'm just saying hi!

ADELE. Hi.

PEG. Hi. You know, I saw you walking into the new Fresh Market, and I said: "Hi, Adele!" And I thought you heard me, but I guess you didn't hear me.

ADELE. I'm in Zumba.

PEG. I'm actually really glad I ran into you again. I'd love to ask you something real quick.

ADELE. I can't really talk. I'm in Zumba.

PEG. I've known you a little while, Adele. You've been to my house for parties. I offered to watch your enormous parrot when you were moving.

ADELE. I can't talk right now. I'm in Zumba.

PEG. I'm not gonna make it in here the whole hour. I'm just trying to get a little information. Something doesn't add up here. And I don't have all the information. You've got to know something about why they just dumped him like that, Adele. Nobody will talk to me. I never had a situation like this. Could you just – maybe you could just come outside for a second?

ADELE. No, I can't.

PEG. What's the big deal? It's one second.

(**PEG** *blocks her path.*)

ADELE. I'm in Zumba. I like being quiet – in Zumba. That's why I love Zumba. Zumba feels like a party, but I don't have to talk to anyone. In Zumba, I can completely tune everything else out and focus on having fun. Because that's a real problem for me, Peg. I've got a problem with finding and experiencing – fun. But, in Zumba, I experience a lot of fun. I don't bring my problems to Zumba because in Zumba, I'm focused on the choreography. And that's why Zumba choreography is so important to me. And right now, I am missing the choreography that is so important to me. So, please. If you need to leave Zumba, you should leave. Zumba isn't for the faint of spirit. If you'd please excuse me, you're in my lane. Please. Move out of my lane!

LOU. Why don't you move out of this lane?

MAPS. Take the long way home to visit your old house in Trenton.

LOU. You know what? It was a prefab house.

ELLA. What's a prefab house?

PEG. Cheap.

LOU. It came on a truck in four pieces. It was kind of neat.

ELLA. I can't turn left here.

LOU. It's okay – just go for it.

ELLA. It's one-way.

LOU. I know! I fought to keep it that way!

ELLA. It's too narrow. I'm turning around.

LOU. Hey, this lady probably lives in our house!

ELLA. Dad, leave her alone!

LOU. I'm going to talk to her.

ELLA. Dad, come on. She doesn't want to talk to you.

LOU. I bet she does!

ELLA. Please leave this person alone.

LOU. Excuse me!

ELLA. Dad! Come on.

MAPS. I'll play this lady on the street. Her power-walking partner canceled today and last week, and the week before that, and she's trying to figure out if it was something she said or what Patricia's fucking damage is.

LOU. Excuse me!

(**MAPS** *steps in as the* **LADY ON THE STREET**.)

LADY ON THE STREET. Can I help you?

LOU. Do you live in that house?

LADY ON THE STREET. Is this a census thing?

LOU. You know what? This is a funny coincidence –

LADY ON THE STREET. Okay. I don't really like funny coincidences.

LOU. So. I actually used to live right there.

LADY ON THE STREET. Okay.

LOU. I lived right there!

LADY ON THE STREET. Okay.

LOU. I planted that cypress tree when my daughter was born. And then I planted that cedar tree when my son was born. But, he had a fatal infant heart condition and only lived for two weeks.

(*A pause.*)

LADY ON THE STREET. Okay. I'm really sorry about that.

LOU. I lived right there from 1984 to 2006.

LADY ON THE STREET. Okay.

LOU. I bet you know Russell Armstrong!

LADY ON THE STREET. Okay. Nope.

LOU. Or maybe his son, what was his son's name – Oscar!

LADY ON THE STREET. Okay. Nope.

LOU. Of course, you do! Oscar had this really popular radio show that played during the morning commute.

LADY ON THE STREET. Okay. I don't listen to the radio. So... No? ...No, thank you?

LOU. You must know the Valentinos!

LADY ON THE STREET. Nope.

LOU. They do the big Halloween decorations?

LADY ON THE STREET. Okay. Nope.

LOU. They do it every single year. I'm sure they still do. If they're still, you know, with us.

LADY ON THE STREET. Yeah. I don't know.

LOU. Oh! Or...um... Aditi and her husband...Steve, I think. They were just moving in when we left... So.

LADY ON THE STREET. Nope.

LOU. Come on – this is a small neighborhood. We've got to know somebody in common!

LADY ON THE STREET. Okay. I've only been here for about four years. So, we wouldn't know each other at all. Bye!

> (**LADY ON THE STREET** *power walks in another direction.*)

LOU. You know what? She wasn't very friendly.

ELLA. I didn't know that. About the trees.

LOU. I did. I planted both of those trees.

MARC. I didn't know that. About the trees.

LOU. I did. I planted both of those trees!

MAPS. It's 1990. Marc comes over for dinner, and you all try not to talk about the baby you recently lost.

MARC. I didn't know you knew how to plant a tree.

LOU. There's a lot of cool things you don't know about me.

PEG. It's not that hard. You just dig a hole, right.

LOU. No, actually, there's a lot more to it than that.

PEG. This corn – is not as sweet as other corn we've had. It's like – mealy.

LOU. We had better corn before. I forget when that was.

PEG. It was supposedly from Amish people. But who knows...

MARC. The meatballs are really good.

PEG. Okay. I won't lie. I can't take credit for that. I cooked them and put the sauce on them, but I did not make them.

MARC. They're really good.

PEG. You want more corn? It wasn't the sweetest.

LOU. Do me a favor and just pop a meatball on my plate?

PEG. If it's not hot enough for you, you might want to heat it up.

MARC. They're really tasty... So, how are you guys holding up?

PEG. We're so sick of our own sad shit – we haven't seen you in a month! Tell us what's new!

MARC. ...I got an offer for the job in Denver.

LOU. Woo hoo! Right on, baby!

MARC. The letter you wrote for me – I'm not this guy, but I teared up a little.

PEG.	LOU.
Awwww.	Shut up. You did not.

PEG. Well, I'm happy for you, but we'll really miss having you guys so close.

MARC. If we go.

LOU. What do you mean if you go? This is the big show! You'll be running your own place! You'd have to wait for three people to croak to get that kind of opportunity around here.

MARC. Karen's not so thrilled about it. She already uprooted her life once for me, and she doesn't think she can do it again. ...I just really don't know what to tell the boys. I got Pierre all excited about learning to ski. But, if I bail on this job in Denver, then forget skiing and maybe forget college too.

PEG. I'll give her a call. I wasn't so thrilled when I moved here, but you adjust.

MARC. I should be able to make a few new hires... You guys could come with us? Make something of a fresh start?

LOU. Oh, that could be very interesting.

(*PEG and LOU check in silently.*)

But Peg just hired two new people and signed a five-year lease on an office.

PEG. It takes a long time to build all the connections you need in my business.

LOU. Now might just not be the best time. Maybe in a couple of years.

MARC. You better come visit. I want to move out in the middle of nowhere and have a lot of space. Maybe some animals.

PEG. Sounds nice.

MARC. You look really good. Did you change your hair or something?

PEG. Maybe I got a little trim.

MARC. It really seems like you're both...doing really well. A lot better.

PEG. He's seeing a good therapist.

LOU. Thanks, Peg. Yes. I am seeing a good therapist.

MARC. Better than seeing a bad therapist.

LOU. We're both doing really well. Peg's got her new nose, and – And this new paper, I really think. This is going to be the best paper I've ever written.

MARC. He says this about every paper.

PEG. Life is so short, you know. I just figured I want the nose I want.

MARC. Absolutely.

PEG. Lou, will you check on Ella, please? I haven't heard a peep.

LOU. She loves that snow globe you got her! I told her we can start a collection. Get one every place we go.

(**PEG** *reaches to* **MARC.**)

PEG. We're really glad to see you. And everything is going to be okay. Alright?

ELLA. I didn't know that about the trees.

(*The scene shifts back to the present.*)

LOU. Yeah, I did. I planted both of those trees.

MAPS. Call Marc and ask for what you need. He and Karen are about to take the tiny horse on the walking path.

LOU. Is now a bad time?

MARC. Actually, yeah, maybe I can call you back – We're about to go out on the walking path.

LOU. It's just a really quick thing.

MARC. We've got Fondue's hair all brushed out and everything.

LOU. The thing is: I'm really interested in Greg's job. The headhunter said they sort of wanted to wrap this up quickly. And...I know you can't tell me, like, exactly where you are in the process, but. I was thinking that, given how competitive this whole thing is – I might need you to really, you know – go to bat for me.

MARC. Well. Yeah. I'm rooting for you.

LOU. You're rooting for me?

MARC. Yeah. I'm rooting for you.

LOU. What do you mean you're rooting for me?

MARC. I just mean I'm rooting for you. There's a whole committee of people involved in these decisions. You know that. But. I'm rooting for you. And if for whatever reason, it doesn't work out here, then I'm still rooting for you. I'm always rooting for you.

LOU. Peg doesn't have all her flower people all lined up anymore, so she can't really just start up the wedding stuff again.

We're putting the house on the market. We'll find a little apartment somewhere...

MARC. That sounds good. You could slow things down a little. You know, there's a lot more to life than just work.

LOU. Says who?

MARC. You could get a great little apartment. You could take up tennis or whatever. You could go visit your cousin down in Florida for a while and hang out on the beach. Hell, I'd like to do the same thing.

LOU. No, you wouldn't. You're just like me. And you wouldn't.

MARC. At some point, I'll be thinking about it.

LOU. But not now. Not when I'm so close to something big. I just need to move and start working as soon as possible. This paper I'm writing, it's really the best paper I've ever written. I don't need any fancy office. I just sort of need a modest, reasonable salary and some lab space – and you'd think – it's pretty simple stuff.

MARC. Hey, I've got to run.

LOU. I forgot to ask you – Is Patrick still in D.C.?

MARC. But please tell everybody I say hello!

LOU. You know – I just saw that great thing about Pierre's computer program, or what, it's like a thing for your phone?

ELLA. Slow down.

LOU. And Paul's baby…give my love to Paul, and Paul's wife – I can't remember her name right now, and the baby, I can't remember her name right now. Have a great holiday weekend. Tell Karen I say hi.

ELLA. Dad, why don't you slow down?

MAPS. You didn't slow down. So. I'll step in as a highway patrol person named Gail. She went into the police force to impress her father, but then her younger sister was the first woman to become a Navy Seal.

> (**MAPS** *steps in as a* **HIGHWAY PATROL PERSON**.)

ELLA. Shit.

LOU. Just be very friendly.

HIGHWAY PATROL PERSON. Good afternoon.

LOU. Good afternoon.

ELLA. Good afternoon.

HIGHWAY PATROL PERSON. Good afternoon.

LOU. Good afternoon.

ELLA. Good afternoon?

HIGHWAY PATROL PERSON. Uh-huh. Good afternoon. Did you happen to see the speed limit sign when you entered Ninety-Five?

LOU. I did see the sign, but I didn't see you, officer!

HIGHWAY PATROL PERSON. Is this your car?

ELLA.	**LOU**.
It's my car.	It's my daughter's car.

HIGHWAY PATROL PERSON. This is your daughter. Mm 'kay. Could I take a look at your license, please?

LOU. Absolutely. My pleasure. I'm just going to reach for my wallet now to happily provide you with my license.

HIGHWAY PATROL PERSON. Thank you for making me feel safe and for saying it's your pleasure.

Could I also see your daughter's registration?

ELLA. I think so...

LOU. You think so?

ELLA. ...I actually don't think so?

LOU. You don't think so?

ELLA. I thought I had it... But what I had turned out to be a corn tortilla.

LOU. YOU HAVE TO HAVE YOUR CURRENT REGISTRATION AND YOUR INSURANCE INFORMATION READY TO GO!

ELLA. Don't yell at me!

LOU. I'M NOT YELLING AT YOU.

ELLA. You're yelling at me!

LOU. YOU CAN'T DRIVE A CAR WITH NO REGISTRATION!

ELLA. Don't yell at me!

HIGHWAY PATROL PERSON. I have to insist that nobody yell at anybody.

ELLA. Officer, I have a small question.

HIGHWAY PATROL PERSON. These eyebrows just run in my family.

ELLA. They're lovely. Would it be a problem right now if I have a lot of parking tickets?

LOU. YOU HAVE A LOT OF PARKING TICKETS?!

ELLA. There's no parking in my neighborhood!

LOU. YOU HAVE TO PAY YOUR PARKING TICKETS!

ELLA. Don't yell at me!

LOU. I'M NOT YELLING AT YOU.

ELLA. You're scaring the dog!

LOU. I'M NOT SCARING THE DOG!

HIGHWAY PATROL PERSON. I need you to calm down, sir. I didn't see the dog there. Hi, dog.

LOU. I'm so sorry, officer. I swear to God I taught her better than this!

I TAUGHT HER TO BE A RESPONSIBLE PERSON WHO PAYS HER PARKING TICKETS AND UPDATES HER REGISTRATION AND WORKS HARD, AND IS WELL-RESPECTED BY HER PEERS. I TAUGHT HER TO BE SOMEONE PEOPLE LOOK UP TO.

HIGHWAY PATROL PERSON. If you can't calm down, I'm going to need you to step out of the car.

LOU. I'm calm. I'm very sorry. The thing is, officer. My daughter is on her way to a very important meeting. She's a very successful person. She wrote a very beautiful little book about giving up. Her current registration is probably packed somewhere in the trunk. We started in Los Angeles, and we're driving all the way across the country. We've seen a lot of amazing things. We'd recommend the Grand Canyon, but you can skip Mt. Rushmore. We just picked up our new dog, Candy. He was a rescue dog, but, well, it's an interesting story. We lost our old dog, Brandy, to laryngeal paralysis. It's a condition when. Well. He wasn't even very old. Only six years old. We thought we had a lot of good years left with him. He had a lot of dental work just the week before he died. He was sort of like, my best friend. He was a little deaf, and he had a little anxiety, but he was really healthy. All of a sudden, he was just panting a lot. Well. He... He couldn't catch his breath. And he.

He just... Collapsed.

(**LOU** *starts to cry.*)

ELLA. Dad, it's okay. It's okay.

LOU. No, it's not.

ELLA. It's just a speeding ticket.

LOU. It's not.

ELLA. Daddy. Come on. It's really just a speeding ticket.

HIGHWAY PATROL PERSON. This is actually just a written warning.

ELLA. Well, look at that! It's just a written warning! Thank you, officer! You're the best! I'd give this traffic stop an excellent rating. Top to bottom. You've been great. See, Dad? Everything is okay!

HIGHWAY PATROL PERSON. When you get a chance, make sure you have your insurance information and your current registration ready to go, like your dad said.

ELLA. Absolutely.

HIGHWAY PATROL PERSON. Uh-huh. I'm going to go. You take care, now.

ELLA. You take care, too!

HIGHWAY PATROL PERSON. Uh-huh. You two take care of each other.

(*The* **HIGHWAY PATROL PERSON** *moves away.*)

LOU. I loved that dog, Elle.

ELLA. I know, Dad.

PEG. I don't understand.

MAPS. Back home in New Jersey, in your mother's kitchen, explain why your father cried over a speeding ticket, which was actually just a written warning.

PEG. I don't understand. Why did he cry?

ELLA. I guess he really loved that dog...

PEG. We all loved that dog but – do you think I should call a doctor?

ELLA. He seems a little better now.

PEG. This dog, though, it's like – he's a genius.

ELLA. I told you.

PEG. Watch this. Candy! Candy-boy – Candy, go get Didi!

ELLA. What's Didi?

PEG. I named the turtle toy Didi. Candy, go get Didi!

(*They watch Candy meander towards a basket on the other side of the room. It takes a while.*)

PEG. Oh my God. See! He goes right to the basket!

ELLA. Yeah – he might be a genius.

PEG. Doggie Genius! Doggie Genius! …Ooo, he likes that! Good boy! Who's my sweet boy?

ELLA. He's so cute. I can't stop kissing him.

PEG. Leave him alone now. He's tired.

ELLA. He's fine.

PEG. Would you like some homemade croutons?

ELLA. Ouch!

PEG. What?

ELLA. They're really hard!

PEG. They're croutons.

ELLA. They're really hard.

PEG. Then don't eat them.

*(**LOU** is on the phone.)*

LOU. Well. I'm glad they thought well of me.

PEG. Shit.

LOU. You guys were great to work with. Very professional. I really enjoyed talking with you. I know you put my best foot forward. Well, I don't want to take up any more of your time. …Hey, listen. I appreciate your call. Okay. Take care. Ha-ha. Okay. Ha-ha. Alright. Have a nice weekend.

   …Something smells good!

PEG. Well. What happened?

LOU. They absolutely loved me.

PEG. Everybody absolutely loves you.

LOU. They thought I was great.

PEG. Everybody thinks you're great.

LOU. But. They picked somebody else.

PEG. Who?

LOU. A woman from Ohio University.

PEG. How old is she?

ELLA. It doesn't matter.

LOU. They said another position may open up in a few years.

PEG. You'll be too old by then.

ELLA. Mom, stop it! It's okay, Dad... Shots on goal, right?

LOU. It's probably for the best, you know? At the end of the day, it wasn't the right fit. They really wanted someone who was more of an administrator, and they really saw that really wasn't where my passion was. It's not really what I'm great at. Marc was really pushing for me... But you know, they had to make a decision.

PEG. Would you like some homemade croutons?

LOU. Ouch!

PEG. What?

LOU. They're really hard!

PEG. Then don't eat them. Maybe I cooked them one minute too long! They're croutons. They're a little hard! But that's the way they are!

LOU. They're good. They're just a little hard.

PEG. Marc should have called you himself. He sends these idiot bounty hunters.

LOU. The headhunters are the ones who call. That's just the way things are done.

PEG. So much for all your fucking friends.

ELLA. Mom!

LOU. Elle, do you need a ride to the train tomorrow morning?

ELLA. I don't think so.

PEG. Yes. You do.

ELLA. I do?

LOU. You've got your big meeting!

ELLA. Oh right. Yeah. I've got that big meeting.

LOU. You should probably bring a couple copies of your resume.

ELLA. Okay, sure.

LOU. I've got some nice paper you can use.

ELLA. Okay. Great.

LOU. I can show you how to print it from my computer.

ELLA. Great.

LOU. You've got your Phi Beta Kappa thing on there, right?

ELLA. No. I do not. Nobody cares about that anymore!

PEG. I don't know why you insist on self-sabotage.

            (**ELLA** *gives* **PEG** *a threatening look.*)

ELLA. Stop.

            (**PEG** *redirects.*)

PEG. Candy, that's cherries! You don't eat cherries.

LOU. You should have your Phi Beta Kappa thing on there. You never know what connection you're going to make when you meet someone.

ELLA. Alright. I'll fix it.

LOU. Good.

ELLA. I'm really sorry, Dad. But there's nothing so great about Denver.

MARC. ...You must have really loved Denver.

MAPS. Ride with your dad to the train station to go to your fake meeting. Wait on the platform until his car turns a corner. Get in a cab towards the airport, put a plane ticket on your credit card, and fly back to Denver.

MARC. Can I get you a café au lait?

ELLA. No, thank you.

MARC. A sliced baguette?

ELLA. No, thank you.

MARC. Some crudités?

ELLA. I just want you to tell me why you didn't hire my dad.

...

LOU. Maybe I'll take the dog for a walk.

PEG. He just had a walk, Lou.

...

MARC. Would you like to feed baby carrots to the tiny horse?

ELLA. He's your best friend, and this is killing him.

...

LOU. Maybe I'll take the dog for a walk.

PEG. He just had a walk, Lou.

...

MARC. I really did my best.

ELLA. You were in a position to help him. And you didn't help him.

MARC. I tried.

ELLA. Try harder.

MARC. Think about it this way: How would you like it if you were up for a job you really deserved...? A job that would be a nice stepping-stone on the path of a nice long career. A job that would make it more possible for you to get another better job, raise your children, make a contribution to your field. And then the old guys in charge, they give it to some other old guy – who has already had a bunch of chances. Just because they're old friends. Just because they went to the same schools and knew all the same people? Isn't that what you're all frustrated about?

ELLA. But I'm talking about my dad.

...

LOU. Maybe I'll take the dog for a walk.

PEG. He just had a walk, Lou.

...

ELLA. All he needs is a building to walk into where people know him and say hi. He just needs somebody who says, "hey, do you know this person who did this thing, and isn't it great that we're all colleagues who know each other?" He deserves that much! He worked on a paper every weekend my whole life. Maybe he won't cure cancer, maybe he won't have a disease or a building named after him, but he is contributing something good to this world, and it's more than most people are doing. And now he's supposed to just, what? Disappear? Sell the house, and then where are they supposed to go?

MARC. He mentioned something about Boston.

ELLA. You're talking like you don't even know these people.

MARC. Look, I'd love to have him here. It would be really fun for me! I called around. I spoke to everybody. I spent a lot of time working on this.

ELLA. It's not good enough.

MARC. I really looked into what was possible. But it just wasn't possible. Right now.

ELLA. It's not good enough!

You made fun of his cowboy boots!

He was the best man in your wedding!

He would do anything for you! And you should be ashamed of yourself!

MARC. Yeah. It's a tough situation.

ELLA. You should be very ashamed!

MARC. But how can I tell people here that I turned down a fantastic, forty-year-old Ecuadorian woman from Ohio, so I could hire my best friend, who, apparently, was accused of harassing his lab assistant.

...

LOU. Maybe I'll take the dog for a walk.

PEG. He just had a walk, Lou.

...

MAPS. Go home and get everything out in the open.

(**ELLA** *hesitates.*)

Go ahead.

LOU. Elle!

PEG. You were gone a long time.

LOU. Ellie! What happened at your meeting?

ELLA. You harassed somebody?

PEG. What do you mean harassed somebody?

ELLA. He said you harassed somebody.

PEG. He didn't harass anybody! He who? Who said that?

ELLA. Marc.

PEG. What is wrong with you, Ella? What's she talking about, Lou?

ELLA. Marc said Dad harassed somebody at work.

PEG. You're shitting me.

ELLA. How does Marc know and I don't?

LOU. ...You talked to Marc?

PEG. How does she know and I don't?

ELLA. Dad...what did you do?

PEG. What did you do, Lou?

LOU. ...I acted a little inappropriately.

ELLA. He said you harassed somebody!

PEG. AND YOU WEREN'T GOING TO TELL ME?

LOU. Peg. She's upset. Just hang on a second.

PEG. I KNEW IT! I KNEW YOU DID SOMETHING.

LOU. Everything's going to be okay.

PEG. No, it's not!

LOU. There's no emergency here. One thing at a time. Elle – what happened at your meeting?

PEG. I'll tell you about her meeting.

ELLA. No! Please. Not right now. I just don't want to do it all right now.

PEG. There was no fucking meeting!

LOU. What happened?

PEG. She didn't have any meeting! Lazy-bones didn't have any meetings with anybody!

LOU. What?

PEG. I MADE IT UP! I MADE IT UP SO YOU WOULDN'T HAVE TO DRIVE ALONE! IT WASN'T GOING TO BE ENOUGH FOR YOU THAT YOUR DAUGHTER WAS WILLING TO DRIVE ACROSS THE COUNTRY TO GET YOUR STUPID DOG!

ELLA. STOP IT! YOU'RE BEING SO MEAN!

PEG. NOW EVERYTHING'S MY FAULT?

LOU. It's nobody's fault.

PEG. WELL, IT'S DEFINITELY YOUR FAULT!

LOU. ...There was never any meeting?

ELLA. No.

But I did send it to a few places.

LOU. Okay. Well.

PEG. We gave her every opportunity in the world, and she did nothing with it.

ELLA. Oh my god. I'm not going to construct my life so it looks impressive to you.

PEG. It doesn't look impressive to anybody.

ELLA. I am trying to do a nice thing! I am trying to be good to you, and you're making it impossible.

LOU. Everyone just take a breath. Everything is going to be okay.

PEG. No, it's definitely not! You'll never get a job! She'll never get a life! We're all just going to keep getting older and older and sadder and sadder. Nothing's ever going to get better. There's nothing to look forward to. You fucked up, Lou. I have no idea how you fucked up so badly.

LOU. Maybe I'll take the dog for a walk.

PEG. He just had a walk, Lou!

LOU. Ellie, you want to come with me?

ELLA. No.

MAPS. Think about it.

LOU. I think I'll take the dog for a walk. Ellie, you want to come with me? Please?

ELLA. No, thank you.

MAPS. Think about it.

LOU. I think I'll take the dog for a walk. Ellie, please come with me?

ELLA. No, thank you. You broke my heart.

MAPS. Okay.

Ella, go back to California. Do your errands and wear your sunscreen.

Lou, follow a green station wagon to the YMCA.

Adele missed her morning Zumba class because her parrot bit her finger. She was going to just cover it with a Band-Aid, but it turns out you really need antibiotics if the saliva of an exotic bird comes into contact with your broken skin. She barely made it to the evening class, which is not her favorite, but if she doesn't make it to Zumba at least four days a week, she starts to lose her grip on reality. Okay. I'll play Adele again.

> (**MARC**, **PEG**, and **ELLA** *dance. They aren't* **MARC**, **PEG**, *and* **ELLA** *in this scene. They are the people who take Zumba at the YMCA.* **LOU** *tries to get* **ADELE**'s *attention.*)

LOU. Adele!

> (**ADELE** *tries not to engage.*)

Adele!

*(**ADELE** continues dancing.)*

Adele!

ADELE. I can't talk.

LOU. Please.

ADELE. I can't talk.

LOU. I just need a couple of minutes of your time.

ADELE. I can't talk.

LOU. I sent you an e-mail.

ADELE. I can't talk. I'm in Zumba.

LOU. I drove over to your house, and I saw you in the driveway, and I said, "Hi, Adele!" And then you got in your car and drove away, and I followed you here. What is this? Some kind of aerobics?

ADELE. It's Zumba.

LOU. Oh. Cool.

ADELE. I can't talk. I'm in Zumba.

LOU. I've known you for a little while. You've been to my house for stuff. My wife offered to watch your parrot, Adele.

ADELE. I can't talk. I'm in Zumba.

LOU. Then, come outside for a second?

ADELE. I can't talk. I'm in Zumba.

LOU. I'm just asking for a bit of decency.

(He grabs her arm to stop her from moving.)

ADELE. DON'T TOUCH ME!

*(The group stops dancing abruptly and stares at him. **LOU** is embarrassed.)*

LOU. I'm so sorry! Are you okay?

ADELE. I'm fine.

(She makes a gesture to show everyone she's fine.)

*(**LOU** and **ADELE** move away from the group.)*

LOU. I shouldn't have touched you. I'm sorry about that.

ADELE. I'm fine.

LOU. Okay. This seems like a cool – what is this again?

ADELE. It's Zumba.

LOU. That's cool.

ADELE. It's very cool.

LOU. You know what? It's pretty simple. I'm having a hard time, Adele. And I just want to apologize for whatever I did, put whatever happened in the past, put it firmly in the distant past.

ADELE. Okay.

LOU. I think I'm really writing the best paper I've ever written, Adele. I think, that if you were able to go to the board of the institute or just write something in an e-mail that says something like:

ADELE. No.

LOU. Please, Adele.

ADELE. No.

LOU. Please, Adele.

ADELE. No.

LOU. Please, Adele.

ADELE. No.

I'm not very active outside of work. It's pretty much just research and Zumba for me. I'm not donating my money to any candidate. I'm not using my personal days for any – community anything. I don't even really do much on the Internet. But, when I thought about it, I realized that one thing I can do – is just try to make sure that smart women like me aren't sabotaged by well-meaning creeps like you.

LOU. What about my wife, who doesn't even know the flower people anymore? What about my daughter, who doesn't even have a dishwasher? I promised I'd take care of them, Adele.

ADELE. Then, you shouldn't have harassed me.

LOU. I'm not even sure what we mean when we use that word.

ADELE. We mean touching my butt two times in Dallas.

LOU. I'm really embarrassed about that. We all had too much fun in Dallas.

ADELE. I wasn't having any fun in Dallas.

LOU. We were celebrating the presentation! We got carried away. We all had too much to drink.

ADELE. I didn't have anything to drink.

LOU. I must have been very tired. I must have been very drunk. I must have been very... I don't know. Overcome.

ADELE. Cathy told me to write everything down.

LOU. What's Cathy got to do with anything?

ADELE. Cathy told me to write everything down.

LOU. Write what down?

ADELE. And what I wrote down was: You put your hand on my butt, and you gave it a strong squeeze. I turned around, and you winked at me. And approximately forty minutes later, you did it again. And I showed what I wrote down to Cathy, and Cathy agreed that you made your choices and that I need to build a wall between my empathy and your culpability.

LOU. I'm very sorry. I'm very embarrassed. Maybe I thought I was being funny. Maybe I thought the joke would land if I did it a second time. I actually don't know what I was thinking.

ADELE. I didn't say anything to anyone except to Cathy. I even laughed as it was happening. Some part of me was flattered, some part of me thought it was just ridiculous. But mostly, I was so humiliated. You're an old married man. You couldn't possibly think I'd be interested in you. And even if you did think that grabbing my ass isn't any path to my hotel room. It's just disgusting juvenile garbage. And so I laughed when I should have screamed. And then I worried all night that my laughter was some kind of invitation. And what if next time, it would be something worse. And what if, in the future, every time I need to ask you a question, I don't. And what if every time we might be the last ones working at night, I leave early. I skipped the goodbye conference brunch in Dallas. I put the whole thing out of my mind, and I focused on my choreography.

LOU. That's great. Look. I'd like to make it up to you.

ADELE. And then, at the next staff meeting, you yelled at me.

LOU. I didn't. I don't remember that.

ADELE. Yes, you do. I cried. I cried in front of Sanjay, and Yoshi, and Lucas, and everyone I work with. Cathy agreed that my work was being undermined, that my confidence was being damaged, and as one of only two women in a department of nine, behavior like yours makes it impossible for me to succeed. Cathy helped me realize that I could spend months or years coming up with different strategies to avoid standing next to you, or I could quietly do something about it right now.

LOU. I'm very, very sorry about what happened in Dallas. You're absolutely right that it was absolutely inappropriate.

ADELE. I know I'm right.

LOU. ...But I didn't really yell at you in the staff meeting.

ADELE. That's not the point.

LOU. Maybe I spoke passionately because I was the lead author on a paper that was the best paper I've ever written, Adele. And you were proposing that I miss my submission deadline while I waited for data that you believed was necessary but wasn't necessary. And, so maybe, I spoke forcefully. Maybe I spoke energetically. Maybe I spoke strongly. But I didn't yell at you. Maybe it sounded that way to you, but I didn't yell at you.

AND YOU KNOW WHAT? SO, WHAT IF I DID YELL AT YOU? ARE WE NOT ALLOWED TO FEEL EXCITED ABOUT SOMETHING? DO WE HAVE TO SIT IN MEETINGS, SIPPING TEA, WITH OUR HANDS FOLDED IN OUR LAPS? DO WE HAVE TO PRETEND LIKE WE DON'T CARE ABOUT ANYTHING? THAT'S NOT HOW PEOPLE GET THINGS DONE, ADELE. I DON'T WANT TO LIVE IN A WORLD WHERE PEOPLE DON'T CARE ABOUT ANYTHING. BECAUSE THAT'S JUST NOT THE TRUTH. THAT'S NOT THE WAY WE ARE, ADELE. WE ARE PEOPLE WHO CARE ABOUT THINGS, ADELE. WE ARE PEOPLE WHO RAISE OUR VOICES WHEN WE CARE ABOUT THINGS, ADELE! I made a mistake in Dallas. But I didn't yell at you.

ADELE. Excuse me. I'm about to miss my favorite song. And my ankle finally healed, so I'm going all out on my turns.

(**LOU** *blocks her path.*)

Let me go.

LOU. Please! I'm begging you.

ADELE. You have to let me go! You stalked me to my Zumba class! You grabbed my arm! You begged me to lie! You are harassing me right now! You don't even realize it! Leave me alone.

(**ADELE** *joins the group in Zumba.*)

LOU. Maybe I'll take the dog for a walk.

PEG. He just had a walk, Lou.

LOU. Maybe I'll take him again.

(**LOU** *and Candy on a walk.*)

(**MAPS** *approaches. She's just* **MAPS** *– not another specific character. She's every friend and neighbor Lou's ever had.*)

MAPS. Beautiful dog.

LOU. Oh, thanks. He's a –

MAPS.	**LOU**.
Rescue.	Rescue.

LOU. My last dog died suddenly of –

MAPS.	**LOU**.
Laryngeal Paralysis.	Laryngeal Paralysis.

MAPS. Terrible disease.

LOU. You look really familiar.

MAPS. So do you!

LOU. I think we went to the same –

MAPS.	**LOU**.
Summer camp.	Summer camp.

LOU. I think our kids were on the same –

MAPS.	LOU.
Swim team.	Swim team.

LOU. I think you used to be my –

MAPS.	LOU.
Dentist.	Dentist.

LOU. You've known me a long time, right?

MAPS. Of course.

LOU. You remember me when I was a little boy, right?

MAPS. Of course.

LOU. Did you ever think that a person like me could end up with so few friends?

MAPS. You've got a pretty good friend right there.

LOU. Well, he's my best friend.

MAPS. You know, what? I recommend anyone considering adoption to consider a senior dog. They already know that when you're restless or you're frustrated, you don't need to tear up a couch or pee on a bed. They appreciate just waking up each day and enjoying whatever they have. But, you know how it is. You volunteered at the shelter with me, so you know.

LOU. I do.

MAPS. Hey, it was great to see you.

LOU. You too. Hey, hope you have a nice holiday.

MAPS. Hey, same to you too.

LOU. Hey, tell Louise I say hi.

MAPS. Hey, I sure will.

LOU. Hey, actually tell Louise I say: Hi Suzanne! She'll know what it means.

MAPS. Hey, that sounds funny.

LOU. Hey, let's get together sometime.

MAPS. Hey, that would be great.

(**MAPS** *stays nearby, watching.*)

LOU. See, Candy, wherever I go, I end up talking to somebody. I had a way of just talking to people.

MAPS. Go inside. Take a shower.

LOU. But I'm so embarrassed...

MAPS. Put on some sweatpants and check the score of the game.

LOU. But all my friends...

MAPS. Go inside. Order a pizza. Help Peg carry a box of dishes down to the basement.

(**LOU** *doesn't move.*)

PEG. Lou, if that dog tracks mud into my house...

MAPS. Go inside. Read the newspaper, write to your cousin who paints the clouds.

(**LOU** *doesn't move.*)

PEG. Lou, if that dog tracks mud into my house...

MAPS. Go inside. Call your daughter in California. Tell her you ran into her old swim coach.

(**LOU** *doesn't move.*)

PEG. Lou, if that dog tracks mud into my house... I'll kill him.

MAPS. Okay.

Kiss your dog.

Send him inside.

*(**LOU** lets the dog go.)*

Take his leash to the garage.

ELLA. ...Wait.

MAPS. Hook it to the pipe on the ceiling.

ELLA. Wait.

MAPS. Place a step stool below the leash.

ELLA. Wait.

MAPS. Step onto the stool.

ELLA. Wait.

Wait. Wait... He can't hang himself.

MAPS. Um.

ELLA. He can't hang himself...with the dog's leash!

MAPS. I haven't quite gotten to that yet.

ELLA. But he loves that dog!

MAPS. I know. I'm sorry. Lou –

ELLA. Stop.

MAPS. Place the loop over your head.

ELLA. I said stop!

MAPS. I'm sorry.

ELLA. Stop saying that.

MAPS. I'm sorry. But, this is the tragedy part.

ELLA. No.

MAPS. He just can't secure a sense of personal dignity.

LOU. I can't.

MARC. No. That's bullshit.

MAPS. He can't reconcile a challenge to his status.

LOU. I can't.

MARC. Yeah. That's bullshit.

MAPS. He tried the whole play, but he can't do it.

LOU. I can't.

MARC. Bullshit.

MAPS. I'm sorry.

ELLA. No. Mom. Do something.

PEG. I can't.

MAPS. You and your mother will never quite recover from this. That's really the tragedy part.

ELLA. No!

MAPS. You'll move home, and you'll take care of each other.

ELLA. No!

I don't want this.

I want to do a comic ending!

I want him to learn something and accept himself in spite of everything!

I'll do anything.

I'll go on a walk!

I'll go to medical school!

Let's do a comedy! Okay?

There should be a celebration! There should be a wedding!

Yes!

Let's do a wedding!

I want to do a wedding!

I want to do a big wedding with lots of flowers and beautiful balloons!

Mom, plan my wedding!

We're having a wedding!

I'll marry anyone you want!

I'll marry anyone who wants to marry me at all!

I'll marry anyone who could tolerate marrying me even a little bit!

MAPS. I could get you some balloons?

ELLA. Okay.

> *(Lots of balloons fall onto the stage.)*

> *(They are very beautiful.)*

Thank you. I hate them.

MAPS. I'm sorry.

ELLA. Mom. Do something!

PEG. ...He fucked up.

ELLA. Dad. Please. We have all these balloons!

LOU. I'm really proud of you.

ELLA. I thought there'd be more time.

MAPS. Lou, why don't you go off to the garage, okay? ...All the way off the stage.

ELLA. Wait! No! I don't want him to. Don't! Please, please, please, please. I'm begging you!

> *(**LOU** leaves the stage.)*

MAPS. Peg, will you play with the dog, please?

PEG. Good boy. You're such a good boy. Who's my sweet boy? No kissing on the face. No. No. No. What did we say about kissing on the face? No kissing on the face.

MAPS. Go back to work. Go back to your little errands and your bright sunny days. Your mother is calling. Answer the phone.

ELLA. I'm just running a little errand. Can I call you when I get home?

PEG. ...Are you sitting down?

MAPS. That's the end. Take the lights out, please.

(The lights go out.)

The End